FINDING HER WORTH

Amish Romance

HANNAH MILLER

Tica House
Publishing

Sweet Romance that Delights and Enchants!

Personal Word from the Author

To My Dear Readers,

How exciting that you have chosen one of my books to read. Thank you! I am proud to now be part of the team of writers at Tica House Publishing who work joyfully to bring you stories of hope, faith, courage, and love.

Please feel free to contact me as I love to hear from my readers. I would like to personally invite you to sign up for updates and to become part of our **Exclusive Reader Club** —it's completely Free to join! Hope to see you there!

With love,

Hannah Miller

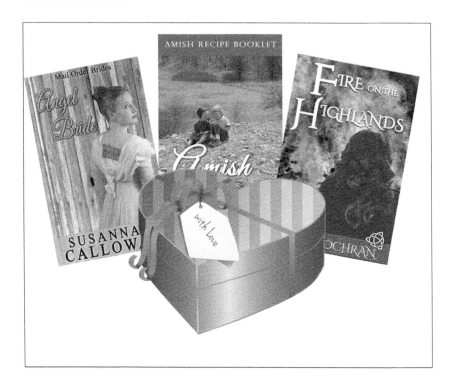

VISIT HERE to Join our Reader's Club and to Receive Tica House Updates:

https://amish.subscribemenow.com/

Chapter One

Iris Glick took a deep breath as she peered into the hand mirror she kept hidden away in her dresser drawer. Over the years, Iris had been told time and time again that she was to only use her mirror to check her curly dark hair and arrange it under her prayer *kapp* – she wasn't to go staring into it for hours on end. But that day, Iris found her *mamm's* strong reprimand did little to keep her from studying her reflection in the piece of glass.

Biting down on her bottom lip, Iris felt like tears might well up as she observed just how homely she truly was. From her thin lips to her too-long nose, she was certainly no beauty.

Goodness, but Iris had been told enough times by her pesky older brother, Ezekiel, that she was ugly, and time was only proving how true his words were. At nineteen-years-old, Iris had surely passed any hope of outgrowing her pitiful looks.

"I'm afraid you're never going to be a beauty, Iris," she whispered to herself as she ran her finger along her reflection and tried to contain her churning emotions.

One of the oldest girls in the Amish community with no beau, Iris could only guess that the local young men were just as repulsed by her looks as she was.

"This has got to stop," she told herself with a resolved sigh. "You've got to show these boys that you're far from worthless. You've got to show them that you're...well..." Iris struggled to find the right words. Honestly, she wasn't sure what she had going in her favor. Certainly, she could cook a good meal, keep a house running, and care for children, but those were tasks every young Amish girl could boast about—not that any of them would consider boasting, however.

In truth, Iris had nothing to set her apart from the other girls.

"Hey..." A banging on Iris's bedroom door startled her, and she gave a slight jump. Before she could answer, the obnoxious voice of her brother continued, "Hey, Long Nose, get on out here... We've got to get going to the youth singing, or we're going to be late."

Iris cringed just at the mention of the young folk's gathering. Every other Sunday night, the unmarried Amish teenagers and young adults would gather at one of the houses to sing and spend time together. As much as Iris wished she could enjoy the events, they tended to only be a bitter reminder that she was alone, and, judging by her looks, always would be.

But Iris wasn't going to let that get her down. Not tonight, anyway. No, tonight she was going to do whatever it took to gain the attention of a boy in the community—any boy.

Since Iris didn't have a boyfriend, she was forced to ride to the singings with her two older brothers, Ezekiel and Thomas. Although both boys were terrible about teasing her, that Sunday night they were more eager to discuss the possibility of Thomas inviting Sally Bontrager to ride home with him.

"Be a lot easier if you didn't have to put up with old Cow Pile back there." Ezekiel snorted as he jerked his head in Iris's direction. Sitting in the back of the black buggy, Iris wished there was some way to get away from her annoying brothers and their biting remarks. So many, many times she had wanted to tattle to her parents about their mean treatment of her, but she never had. She wasn't certain why she hadn't. Maybe she was afraid it would get worse if she tattled.

She didn't know of any other brothers in the entire district who were so mean to their sisters.

She sighed. She needed to stick up for herself. Once and for all.

Well. Maybe she would. If she could grab a boy's attention tonight, anything could happen. Anything at all.

Leaning her chin against the palm of her hand, Iris closed her eyes and tried to ignore the conversation her brothers were having. She had no interest in hearing about their plans to talk to girls, and anything they might say toward her would only be hurtful in the long run.

By the time they arrived at the young folk's gathering, Iris's decision to gain the attention of any boy had grown more pressing and more urgent.

Henry Rupp gave the horse a final rub and then wiped his hands against his black pants legs. While Henry's family did no chores on Sunday, there was always the need to feed the horses. With his parents busy preparing for the singing about to take place in their home, Henry had tended to all the animals. He didn't mind – he rather enjoyed the chance to spend time with the animals.

Glancing out the barn door, Henry could see that the Amish youth were already starting to pour into the yard, their buggies like black hulks against the lush green lawn. Henry smiled to himself as he leaned against the barn door and watched them continue to arrive, one after another. Raising a hand, he greeted the approaching teenagers.

He glanced up just in time to see Thomas Glick pull his horse to a stop next to the barn and battled a sick feeling in the pit of his stomach. Watching as both Thomas and Ezekiel left their sister struggling to get out of the buggy without dropping a covered dish, Henry had to grit his teeth in annoyance.

There had been a time when he and Thomas had been what some would consider close friends in school. Snorting at the idea now, Henry had to realize those days were long gone. While Thomas had never done anything directly to Henry, the way he and his younger brother treated Iris was more than Henry could stand.

Deciding it was wrong to leave Iris to try to fumble on her own, Henry sucked in a deep breath and started across the lawn toward the buggy.

"If you'd get down, we'd be able to get the horse unhitched," Ezekiel was griping as Henry drew closer to the recently arrived siblings.

Iris let out a discouraged sigh as she tentatively lowered her foot to step down, a huge pan of brownies held precariously in her hands, giving her no way to catch herself if she fell.

"Here," Henry spoke up as he stepped next to the wagon and offered his hand. "Let me take those for you."

Taking the plate of brownies in his hands, Henry offered the young woman his elbow so she could grab it and lower herself to the ground.

For a moment, Henry wondered if Iris was going to accept his invitation. Slowly, she reached out and clasped onto his arm as she climbed down from her place in the buggy.

"Well, it's about time." It was Thomas's turn to throw a harsh comment her way. Turning to look at Henry, Thomas added, "Sorry about that, Henry. You'd think she would have learned how to get in and out of a buggy by now, but she's always been a little slow."

Iris immediately let go of Henry's arm and reached for the dish of brownies. As Henry passed the pan of delicious treats her way, he couldn't ignore the fact that her face looked red with embarrassment, and her eyes appeared like she might have been crying earlier.

Not pausing to give him a second look, she turned and started toward his parents' house.

Henry had to swallow a lump of mingled irritation and heartbreak as he turned toward Thomas and asked, "Do you have to be so rough on her?"

"Rough?" Thomas asked with a laugh as he worked on the horse's bridle.

"On Iris," Henry returned, his voice almost getting caught in his throat, "She is a person, you know. A person made in the image of *Gott*. And not only that, but she's also your sister.

Surely, you and Ezekiel could learn to show her a little bit of respect."

Thomas rolled his eyes, and Henry could see Ezekiel give a sneer.

"Henry, Henry, Henry," Thomas reached out and gave Henry a slap on the arm accompanied by a condescending sigh, "I tend to forget that you have no sisters. Believe me, if you had a sister, you'd know what we put up with. Ezekiel and I just like to tease her a little bit...it makes her tougher. She doesn't mind."

Ezekiel was nodding his head as he reached up to wipe a stream of sweat off his forehead with the corner of his sleeve.

Realizing his words were falling on deaf ears, Henry shook his head and started toward some of the other young folk. Whether the Glick boys truly believed their words were meaningless or not, Henry would have no luck changing their hearts. That was a job that would have to be reserved for the good Lord alone. Henry would pray that the boys' consciences would be pricked, but he could do little else to change Iris's sad situation.

Chapter Two

Standing by the snack bar inside the Rupp's spacious farmhouse, Iris reached for another cookie and gobbled it right down.

"You like those, don't you?" The cheerful voice of Iris's friend, Lydia, never failed to bring a smile to her face.

Turning to look at Lydia, Iris nodded. "Sure do. These might be the best cookies I've ever had."

"No surprise there," Lydia returned with a grin of her own. "Since I made them."

The backdoor swung open and a stream of young men came pouring into the room. Sweaty from the heat of the afternoon, they hit the snack table with a vengeance.

"Better be careful eating so many cookies," Ezekiel warned Iris as he grabbed a handful of goodies for himself. "You don't want to end up chunky on top of everything else."

Iris listened as her brother chortled at his own joke and felt like she might be sick to her stomach. Looking away from him, she attempted to ignore his presence entirely.

Just as fast as the boys had hit the table, they were gone, heading back outside to try to get in a few moments of visiting before it became dark and they were called indoors to sing.

"Rotten brothers," Iris muttered under her breath as she stared down at the floor, still too ashamed to meet the sympathetic stare of Lydia.

"You eat as many cookies as you want." The smooth voice broke into her thoughts, alerting Iris that she and Lydia were not alone after all.

Looking up in surprise, Iris stared into the sea-blue eyes of Jason Rutger. While Jason and his family were new to the community, Iris had seen him at several of the recent singings. But this was the first time he'd ever acted like he noticed her.

"Don't pay any attention to those boys," he continued. He allowed his eyes to travel up and down Iris, taking her in completely as he went on. "You're beautiful just the way that you are."

Iris felt her cheeks flush as she stammered, trying to say something appropriate in reply to his words. She'd never heard such an outright compliment in her entire life—not aimed at her or anyone else for that matter. "I...well...I...."

Lifting a finger, Jason stilled her words by suggesting, "How about you sit across from me during the singing tonight?"

Still unable to speak, Iris simply nodded her head.

Smiling at her obvious discomfort, Jason gave a wink and headed toward the door to join the others outside.

As soon as he disappeared, Lydia stepped up closer to Iris and let out a worried sigh as she warned, "*Ach*, Iris. Haven't you heard what's been going around about Jason Rutger? Some folks are saying that his family had to move here because...well, because he and some girl back in Indiana had...um... They called it a scandal. Some folks are mighty wary of him."

Iris shook her head and set her jaw before replying. "Lydia, rumors are just that—rumors. I-I'm paying no attention to them."

But deep in her heart, Iris wondered whether the rumors might hold more truth than she wanted to admit. However, at that moment, she wasn't about to diminish the first outright nice thing she'd heard in a long while—and she was willing to do just about anything to block out the criticism of her brothers.

Jason had said that she was beautiful. Not that she believed it, of course, but no one had ever told Iris Glick that before.

Iris felt like her heart was going to beat right out of her chest when the young folks began to pour into the house and gather around the long wooden table to sing some of their favorite old hymns. She scanned the room for Jason, hoping against all hope that someone wouldn't have stolen the seat directly across from him. She wasn't sure what she would do if she missed out on her chance to be close to the handsome young man.

Iris bit back her smile of pleasure when she saw that the chair across from Jason was, indeed, still empty. Looking closer, she saw that he'd stretched out his legs and rested his feet on the seat.

Ach, was he saving the seat for her? The mere thought of it brought a distinct heat to her cheeks. For so many years, she had watched her friends be courted by young men in the community. Iris had always been the one who'd been forced to sit alone...unwanted and unsought after by anyone in her church district.

But, tonight, it looked like that was all about to change. Iris was determined to do whatever it took to keep the attention of Jason Rutger and to prove she was more than simply her unfortunate looks.

Making her way a group of giggling girls, Iris reached the spot across from Jason and put her hand on the back of the wooden chair.

"Is this spot still available?" she asked, her voice almost getting caught in her throat as she tried to sound more confident than she felt.

Jason looked up at her with a flash in his eyes, and then he gave a shrug and explained, "Of course it's available. I've been saving it for you."

Feeling the heat start to rise to her cheeks once again, Iris could only hope she appeared more certain of herself than she actually felt. Lowering herself into the seat, she forced herself to look across the table at Jason and give him what she hoped was a fetching smile.

Jason gazed back, his blue eyes practically boring holes into her. It felt as if he could see straight into her soul, and the sensation was totally unnerving, yet she fought to keep up her brave front. Rather than looking away, she continued to look directly into his gaze.

The other young people started to file into their places; however, Iris paid little attention to the chairs and the benches that were scooting out and in around her as the other girls scurried to find spots. Instead of noticing the girls around her, she continued to look at Jason Rutger.

Finally, Jason's expression relaxed and, rather than continuing to study her seriously, he allowed a slight, mischievous grin to play across his lips. For a moment, Iris was almost frightened at what his look could mean, but she didn't allow herself to dwell on her fears. If she ever intended to find love and have a family of her own, she was going to have to do whatever it took to get close to a boy. If that meant being a bit forward and bold, then she would force herself to do just that.

Gathering all of her courage, she forced an unwavering smile to her face and kept it fixed on Jason. The moment between them was interrupted as Henry Rupp's father, Sam, took his place at the head of the table and began to call out the upcoming songs for the night.

As Iris allowed her voice to carry some of the familiar old hymns, she felt like her heart was going to float right out of her chest. For the first time in her life, a boy was paying attention to her, and she was going to make sure that he found her interesting.

Sitting at the far end of the table, Henry Rupp's gaze continuously traveled toward Iris Glick. Henry had tried his best to stick up for her and had done his part to shame her brothers into behaving, but he doubted his words would ever do any good.

Turning slightly so he could see Ezekiel and Thomas, Henry had to swallow hard to keep from getting angry as he watched the older boys nudging each other and whispering during the songs. The two were certainly a disgusting pair of boys. Henry didn't know how they could possibly be Iris's brothers, not when she was so nice.

In his opinion, Ezekiel and Thomas were obnoxious, loud, arrogant, and completely unconcerned about anyone other than themselves. And dear Iris... Henry could remember from their time together in school that Iris was always the quiet one who kept to herself. Never once had Henry heard her speak a harsh word about anyone, nor had she ever done anything to hurt another human being as far as he knew. Instead, she simply played alone and apparently tried to avoid others.

Henry could remember times when he'd tried to include her in games, but he'd quickly found that talking to Iris Glick was just asking for rejection. No matter how kind Henry tried to be, Iris only pushed him away, ignoring his attempts completely.

As he forced himself to belt out more notes to his favorite song, Henry's heart was heavy. He had to do something to help Iris. The idea of her having to endure a buggy ride home with those disgusting brothers was more than he could stomach. No, Henry would risk rejection again and step forward to offer a hand in friendship. If he was rejected again, then it was simply a burden he would have to bear. It was becoming clearer and clearer to him that Iris was too valuable to be treated so poorly.

Nodding his head, Henry became resolved with his decision. He was going to ask Iris Glick to let him drive her home in his buggy.

Chapter Three

Throughout the evening, Iris continued to catch Jason studying her, his eyes traveling across her face and down her neck. Sometimes his attention made her feel uneasy and yet she forced herself to remain calm.

Iris was certain the other girls around her were also noticing the looks Jason sent her way, and, while it made her a bit uncomfortable, she also felt a sense of pride. For the first time, she was the center of attention for a boy.

And what a boy. Jason was one of the best-looking boys in the district.

When the singing ended and Sam Ruff announced it was time for the young folk to start heading home, Iris found her stomach in a swirl of butterflies.

"Iris?" Lydia called, bringing her to her senses and forcing her attention off Jason. Lydia held a measure of apprehension in her dark eyes as she studied Iris, occasionally darting a glance in Jason's direction as if she were afraid of what he might do next.

"What?" Iris asked.

"I just wanted to see if you would like to ride home with me and Lucas? You're on our way, and neither of us would mind one bit."

While Iris appreciated her friend's obvious attempt at saving her from a miserable ride home with her brothers, she wasn't going to intrude on Lydia's time with her beau.

Shaking her head, Iris forced a smile and started to speak but was interrupted.

Jason Rutger had come around the table and was now standing right next to her, so close she could easily reach out and touch him if she moved her hand only a fraction of an inch.

"Iris Glick." Jason held his hat between his hands and watched her coolly, his voice strong and sure. "I wondered if the sweetest girl in the district would do me the honor of letting me take her home?"

Iris swallowed around the tightness that was forming in her throat. She noted that several of the other girls were eyeballing her from a distance, looks of obvious jealousy splattered across their faces as they watched the handsome new boy talk to her.

Iris tried to look as casual as she shrugged shyly and replied, "I suppose the sweetest girl wouldn't mind too much...as long as you're a gentleman."

Iris was stunned at the ease with which the coy words slipped from her lips. She watched an amused smirk cross Jason's face, and he nodded in return. "*Jah*, I think I might be able to act like a gentleman...at least this once." Raising an eyebrow, he added, "But I'm not very good at behaving."

Fighting a grin of her own, Iris lowered her voice to return, "Then maybe I shall force you to learn."

The words must have seemed like a challenge to Jason for he smiled broadly. He reached out to softly touch the small of her back and whispered, "Meet me outside in about ten minutes. I have to go hitch up the buggy."

Watching Jason leave the house to go into the dark coolness of the summer night, Iris found herself trembling with anticipation and nerves. She couldn't believe she'd finally been invited to go on a buggy ride with a young man. Not only that, but she could tell that Jason was intrigued with her. She wondered why, but she refused to let herself dwell on that and ruin everything.

While Iris might not be the sweetest girl in the community, she could do her best to ensure she was the most exciting. If some teasing and flirting was what it took to keep the attention of Jason Rutger, then she would do everything in her power to become a professional at it.

"Goodness, Iris." Lydia stood nearby, frozen in place with her jaw open in disbelief. "What was *that?* I've never seen you act so bold around a boy before."

Determined not to let her friend make her feel badly about it, Iris squared her shoulders and declared, "You're about to see a new Iris." Raising her chin, she continued, "I'm done being the girl who hides in the corner and is completely ignored. It's time for something different." Her words sounded bold, even if Iris wasn't really sure what they entailed. Nor was she even sure that she meant them.

Lydia didn't look at all approving as she shook her head, the strings on her prayer *kapp* fluttering over her shoulders. "I'm just don't think..."

Lydia's impending warning was interrupted as a familiar deep voice spoke up to say, "Iris...I have a question for you."

Turning on her heel, Iris stared into the face of Henry Rupp. He was nervously shifting from one foot to another, rocking his weight back and forth as if he were hardly able to stand his ground.

Lowering his dark eyes to the floor, he asked, "I was wondering if you might want...or if you might need—"

"Iris," Jason had re-entered the room and pushed right past

Henry, practically knocking the other boy over in his enthusiasm to get to her side. "Iris, *kumm*...the buggy is hitched, and I'm ready to take you home."

Iris found her gaze magnetized to Henry, and she had to force herself to look away from him to focus on Jason.

"I'll be right there," she told him. Then she turned her attention back to Henry to ask, "What were you saying, Henry?"

Suddenly, it seemed that Henry had retreated. He shook his head, looked uncomfortable, and stepped back, as if he were admitting defeat. Giving what looked like a fake smile, he replied, "Nothing, Iris. Nothing at all. Just have a *gut* night and be safe."

Allowing Jason to take her by the elbow, Iris let him lead her outside toward his awaiting buggy. She turned back to give Lydia a smile, and she ignored her friend's concerned look.

For the first time in nineteen years, Iris was being pursued by guy. She wasn't going to allow anyone to destroy it for her.

Sitting beside Jason on his buggy seat, Iris tried to enjoy herself. But despite her best efforts, she found her thoughts continually trailing back to Henry Rupp.

What was he going to ask her? Why had he come over to talk

to her, only to retreat when Jason showed up? Could it be that Henry had wanted to ask her to ride home with him?

As soon as the thought crossed her mind, Iris shoved it away. It was ridiculous to even think such a thing. After never having any boy ask to escort her home, why in the world would there be two asking on the same night?

Iris had known Henry her entire life – growing up alongside him and going to school with him. While Henry had always been friendly and kind to her, Iris had always known he was simply trying his best to be sympathetic. He hated to see her slighted, and Iris appreciated it.

But something about knowing that Henry only looked at her as a pathetic service project hurt Iris. On her own part, she'd always thought of Henry as so much more than just an acquaintance – she'd always wished they could share more together. Of all the boys in the community, Henry was the one Iris wished was her beau.

But that was not to be. Not with Iris as downright unattractive as she knew herself to be. No, there was no chance Henry would ever give her a second look, despite his kindness. Otherwise, he would have made a move much sooner.

"So..."

Iris jumped when Jason spoke up, practically whispering in her ear as he moved his body over closer to hers.

"Am I being a good enough boy so far?"

Iris smiled at his question. There was something about his lighthearted way of talking that helped her put her troubling thoughts aside. Jason was certainly a distraction from the pain of her daily life, and Iris was going to take full advantage of the time she had with him.

Giving a shrug, she forced herself to once again be coy as she replied, "*Jah*, so far, I'd say you get an A."

"Oh." Jason laughed. "So, it's now a test, huh?" Lowering his voice slightly, he added, "I've never done very good on tests. I almost hate to ruin my bad reputation."

Something about his words made Iris feel like jumping from the buggy seat and running away. She wasn't sure if she was cut out for this kind of teasing with a boy.

"What if I do this?" Jason whispered as he moved a little closer and draped an arm across one of her shoulders, bending so close to her ear that she could feel his hot breath against her skin.

Sucking in a gush of the warm night air, Iris replied, "*Ach*, I'd say that you're getting down to a low B now."

Growing increasingly uncomfortable with the feel of him so close to her, Iris sat up straighter and asked, "Can this horse go any faster?" Rushing to give some reason for her comment, she added, "My pokey brothers rarely do more than a slow clop with our buggy."

Jason relaxed and pulled away from her, laughing out loud as he announced, "Iris Glick, I don't know what to make of you." Once he had calmed his chuckles, he continued, "This horse surely can go faster. I just didn't know if you'd like it or not."

Smiling impishly, Iris hoped she looked somewhat appealing as she assured him, "I've always had a soft spot for going quick-like."

Taking up the challenge, Jason urged his horse forward, speeding it up until the buggy was practically flying down the calm country road.

Iris had to clasp the edge of the seat with both hands to steady her nerves as he careened the buggy forward.

In all honesty, Iris had never been a fan of going fast; however, it had certainly sounded adventurous. She guessed that adventure and excitement were two reasons that Jason Rutger might keep looking her way. If she wanted to keep his attention, she was going to have to make sure to provide both.

Iris only hoped she could continue to come up with ways to prove herself exciting that didn't involve getting closer physically. While she thought Jason was a handsome young man, the way he touched her unnerved her in every way possible.

Past warnings from her mother filled her thoughts. Her *mamm* had always told her she had to be wary of boys who wanted to put their hands on her. Kissing and snuggling weren't to be taken lightly. Up until this point, it had never been an issue, since no one had ever wanted to come within a yard of Iris, but Jason was far too grabby for Iris's comfort.

Yet no matter what, Iris knew she would be willing to stretch her own comfort to keep Jason interested in her—and her, alone.

Chapter Four

Sitting at the desk in his bedroom, Henry Rupp allowed his gaze to travel out the window to the ground outside. The trees and the moon worked together to create eerie shadows on the lawn. The entire night, which had started out so well, now seemed overwhelmed with an ominous sense.

"Iris..." Henry spoke the girl's name into the emptiness of his bedroom.

Then he shook his head, disgusted that he was allowing his thoughts to travel down this dangerous path.

"I was trying to be nice to her, but she didn't need me," he told himself aloud. "That's all that happened. I wanted to keep her safe from her brothers, but Jason had already made a way for her to get home."

Even as Henry considered the new boy in the community, his heart gave a lunge. He didn't know much about Jason Rutger, but during the little bit of time they had spent in the same vicinity, Henry had to admit that Jason seemed to be a loud, conceited, and unruly young man. Rumors were already circulating that Jason had led an unsavory life before moving to their district, and while Henry tried not to pay too much attention to gossip, there was usually some truth to the tales that passed through their Amish grapevine.

Closing his eyes, Henry leaned his head against his hand and allowed himself to whisper a prayer into the emptiness of his room, "Please, *Gott*, please keep Iris safe. Protect her in every way possible. Amen."

All in all, Iris had to admit that her first night spent riding with Jason Rutger lacked a sense of depth she longed for deep in her heart. While Jason provided an opportunity for her to escape the ridicule of her brothers, he wasn't all that appealing as an individual.

During their time together, they had very little to say to each other apart from flirtations and goofy jokes.

If Iris had hoped that things would get better with time, she was in for a sorry surprise. While she continued to accept rides to and from social events with him, the time spent together grew less and less enjoyable.

"Why are you so quiet tonight?" Jason asked one evening as he drove her toward the youth sing at the Lapp homestead.

Shrugging, Iris hoped he wouldn't notice how pensive she truly was. While she didn't particularly enjoy Jason, just having a young man pay attention to her meant more than she could begin to explain. She had come to depend on his presence in her life over the last few weeks and found his attention gave her a sense of significance she couldn't find anywhere else.

"It's nothing," she assured him with a forced smile before she thought up a teasing comment. "I just wanted to make you work at getting me friendly tonight."

Jason's face grew dark, and he suddenly looked overcome by an emotion that Iris could hardly place.

Scooting closer to her, Jason reached behind to put a hand on the small of her back as he whispered, "Is that so? Is it time for me to start working for things? Because I can be a pretty hard worker when it's for something I want."

The buggy was now slowing, and Iris felt like she might grow sick to her stomach. She tried to think of some kind of silly reply that might distract him from his intent, it was difficult for her mind to stop spinning long enough to think.

Pulling the buggy to a total stop, Jason turned on his seat and pulled Iris closer to him. He placed his finger gently on her lip and leaned forward until his face was only inches away from hers. "Do you want me to teach you some new things? Things more fun than just riding fast in buggies?"

Swallowing hard, Iris couldn't fight her discomfort any longer. Pulling away from him, she sharply replied, "*Nee*, Jason. Not at all. Goodness, but this isn't right. You know we shouldn't be doing such things."

As if he'd been doused with ice water, Jason jerked away from her. Grabbing the reins in both hands, he replied, "Fine then."

Studying his face, Iris was sure she had ruined the evening.

"I thought that you wanted to have fun, Iris," he said. "I thought you and I wanted the same things...but now, I'm beginning to wonder if maybe we're too different."

"Too different?" Iris repeated, her voice sounding small. "What do you mean, too different?"

Jason shook his head and replied. "Well, just look at you for one thing. Acting all prudish all of a sudden. I guess I just need time to think."

The next few miles of the trip were made in silence with Jason staring straight ahead, an ugly scowl on his face. With each turn of the wheels, Iris wondered if she had destroyed any chance of a relationship with Jason. For the first time in her life, Iris finally had a boy paying attention to her and now...well, now she had gone and messed it all up.

"Jason?" Iris sucked in a deep breath and reached out to put a hand on top of his.

Jason instantly turned to look at her, something akin to hope in his eyes. He slowed the buggy to a stop and pulled into an empty patch of dirt alongside the road.

Swallowing hard and making herself do it, Iris nodded and muttered, "Perhaps I spoke too soon. I'm sorry... I just thought that it would be fun to tease you for a bit." She could only hope that her beau would buy the lie.

Whether he believed her or not, Iris wasn't sure, but Jason's scowl was instantly replaced by a smirk. Leaning forward, he repeated, "Tease me, huh?"

In a moment, he had overtaken her with a kiss that felt overwhelming, forceful, and controlling. Rather than enjoy it, when she finally pulled away, Iris felt almost sullied...as if she had been used rather than kissed.

"Did you like that?" Jason asked, a cocky expression on his face. "How did I grade on that one?"

"It-it wasn't bad," Iris returned, trying her best to seem as light-hearted. "Although you may have to do it again if you want me to grade you proper-like."

Ach, but why in the world had she said that?

As Jason went in for another kiss, Iris tried to enjoy it. She knew other girls had kissed their beaus. They never spoke of it much, but when they did, they made it seem pleasant and enjoyable. All she felt was nasty about herself and about the things she was doing. Yet, at the same time, she would feel even worse if she had to go back to being the lonely girl who was overlooked by everyone.

Watching Iris Glick descend from Jason Rutger's buggy, Henry Rupp felt his insides give a flip deep. There was something about seeing her arrive to singings every other week with that wretched boy that made Henry feel continuously worse. He honestly didn't know what Iris saw in him.

Leading his horse toward the barn, Henry could only hope he could unhitch his animal and get away before he had to be around Jason. Working to get the bridle off the horse, Henry inwardly groaned when he heard someone in the barn call out, "Hello there, Jason."

Glancing behind him, Henry watched as Jason led his buggy right up to the side of his. A wide grin was on the young man's face, but he looked almost evil as he nodded toward Henry.

"How's it going, Jason?" someone called out to ask.

Jason chuckled as he replied, "Going *gut*, boys. Going *gut*. I just had quite the ride over here with Iris Glick. I think I'm going to start calling her my little firecracker." Before anyone could ask what he meant, Jason hurried to explain, "I kid you not, boys...that girl is something else. I, well, I'm surprised that no one has snatched her up, if you know what I mean."

Henry sucked in a deep breath and turned his back so no one would see his anger. Jason's words were so crass and vulgar that Henry thought he could actually hit him.

"Iris?" Ben Miller asked, his voice incredulous, "Iris Glick? She's never let anyone even get close to her."

Jason gave a shrug and snorted. "What can I say? I guess I have the magic touch."

Pulling his buggy back and situating it closer to the barn, Henry wiped his hands on his pant legs and started toward the house where the singing would soon take place. He couldn't stand to hear such loutish comments about Iris for another moment.

He could only hope Jason's stories were exaggerations.

Chapter Five

Standing next to her friend in a corner of the Lapp home, Iris found it hard to keep her thoughts from traveling in troubling directions. Now that she had kissed Jason and pretended to like it, how would she ever be able to stop him in the future? Likely, he would expect her to kiss him again...and who knew what else?

"Iris," Lydia said, her voice sounding sympathetic, "you look awful pale tonight. Are you okay?"

Nodding her head, Iris tried to look more pleasant than she felt. "*Jah*. Of course, I'm okay. Maybe just a bit tired."

Glancing around the room almost as if she wanted to ensure that no one would hear their conversation, Lydia lowered her voice to ask, "Did you ride with Jason again?"

The question seemed almost ridiculous. "You know I did, Lydia. We've been riding together for weeks now."

Iris couldn't ignore the fact that Lydia sobered as she looked down at the floor and whispered, "Iris, I don't know how to tell you this, but you need to think long and hard about the time that you're spending with him. Before things turn serious, please consider what you're doing. He's...well," she stumbled on the words, "he's not a very nice boy, to be honest. The things he says to the other boys...well, they're right-down vulgar. In fact, my Lucas is getting so tired of it, he can hardly stand to see Jason coming. Some of the young men are even thinking of having a conversation with the bishop."

Feeling her discomfort growing by the second, Iris squirmed. "The bishop? I hardly think that's necessary. And I don't know what you're talking about. Jason is always a gentleman with me." The lie tumbled from her mouth before she could stop it. Shame burned through her. What was she doing? Lydia was her dear friend. Why in the world should she be lying to her?

Lydia frowned. "I don't want to tell you this, I really don't. But...some of the things that Jason has been saying are about you. And I have a feeling that the bishop is going to want to talk to you along with Jason if he finds out what is being said. And if not the bishop, then the deacons, at least."

Iris felt her blood run cold. What was Jason saying about her?

Was he making things worse than they actually were? Up until recently, the two of them had not even kissed. Surely, he wouldn't try to make it sound like they were doing more.

"Please, Iris," Lydia begged as she reached out and tried to take her friend's hand in her own. "Don't let him do this to you. Don't let him ruin your reputation and do things that he shouldn't...you're better than this."

Jerking her hand away, Iris could stand it no longer. "You don't understand, Lydia. You don't know what it's like to be ugly and unwanted. For the first time in my life, someone is interested in me, and I'm not going to let that fall apart. Jason cares for me and me alone, and I will do whatever it takes to ensure that he continues to do just that."

Before Lydia could say anything else, Iris turned on her heel and marched away, making a bee-line toward a corner on the other side of the room.

Despite Iris's best efforts at ignoring Lydia's words, they continued to play in her mind during the ride home and into the week. She thought about asking Jason what he was saying about her but decided better of it.

During their time together, Iris had learned to rely on the feelings she got from Jason. He was the only person who made her feel pretty and desirable. She couldn't risk losing that...not now. The idea of going back to the hole of loneliness and despair was more than she could bear.

"You sure are quiet tonight," Jason announced as he guided his horse down the road on an evening ride. "Although, maybe you have a lot more on your mind than talking."

Iris swallowed hard as she considered his comment – she certainly did have a lot more on her mind than simple chit-chat.

"Jason," she started slowly, wishing she could somehow make him understand the uncertainties that were swirling in her mind. Where were things with Jason truly going? Was there any hope she might be able to truly have a life with him? While she didn't care for Jason in the way she should a husband, it was beginning to seem like he was her only chance at ever having a family of her own.

"Jason?" She sat up straighter and forced the words out. "I was wondering if you'd like to start spending some more time together than mainly our trips back and forth to youth events. How would you feel about coming to my parents' house for supper tomorrow night? It would give you a chance to spend time with my whole family. I know it might be considered a bit unconventional, but still, I think it might be nice."

The words were hardly out of Iris's mouth before Jason began to furiously shake his head, almost as if he couldn't rid himself of the suggestion quickly enough.

"*Nee*," he replied firmly, "I can't. I've got things to do."

His total refusal stabbed Iris deeper than she wanted to admit. Leaning back against the buggy seat, she could only hope she could stop the tears from coming to her eyes.

Obviously sensing her reaction, Jason reached across the distance between them to put a hand on her arm as he assured her. "Come on, Iris. Don't be sad. I can't stand to see you sad. If I didn't have somewhere that I had to go for work with my dad's driver, then I would for sure and for certain come to your house for supper." Giving her a wink, he added, "We'll have plenty of time for family gatherings in the future. For now, let's just enjoy the present."

While Iris tried to rest assured that him talking about their future was a good thing, it was hard for her to push aside an uneasy feeling that Jason didn't plan to stick around in her life for much longer.

"Come on, Iris. I bet I can beat you to the general store." Lydia's cheerful voice rang out into the clear summer evening.

While Iris had been completely put out with her friend at the singing, Lydia had come to visit her Monday afternoon and had quickly made things right between them. Both the girls apologized and made a pact that they would never again allow a boy to come between them.

Lydia stayed for supper and then, after the meal was over, suggested they ride their scooters to the Amish general store in town to pick up some fabric for a quilt they were going to start working on together.

Iris laughed at her friend's suggestion that they race. She was grateful that the bishop had allowed the scooters. Balancing on them was fun, and when she pushed off with her foot, she could get quite a speed going. Grabbing her scooter, she jumped onto it and called out, "I wouldn't be so sure about you beating me."

Pushing her black shoe against the ground over and over, she careened toward the store, laughing as she enjoyed the peace of the evening. She was thankful to finally have an opportunity to put her troublesome thoughts about Jason out of her mind.

Almost as if appreciating the moment had jinxed her, she pulled her scooter to a stop outside the general store but hesitated behind the corner when she recognized Jason's familiar black buggy clipping down the street.

"What are you doing?" Lydia asked as she pulled to a stop beside her.

"Shhh." Iris held a finger to her lips and motioned her head toward his buggy. "There goes Jason."

She couldn't ignore the fact that Lydia rolled her eyes before she could catch herself and get her reaction in check.

"Where could he be going?" Iris asked herself as much as Lydia. "I thought he was supposed to be busy with work this evening."

Iris's mind traveled in a dozen different directions. Why was her beau out riding in his buggy when he was supposed to be going somewhere with a paid driver? Before she could gather her good sense, Iris grabbed tightly onto the handles of the scooter and boldly declared, "I'm going to follow him."

"Iris..." Lydia let out a groan and started to speak as if she would try to convince Iris otherwise.

But before Lydia could change her mind, Iris started off down the street, following Jason's buggy at break-neck speed.

Lydia came after her, pushing her foot against the pavement to gather speed for the ride.

Jason's buggy was just a blob in the distance, but Iris wasn't going to give up. She continued to push against the pavement, making her way over the asphalt. The buggy continued to travel farther and farther down the road until the farms gave way to the barren countryside.

"Iris!" Lydia called out with a huff as she tried to catch her breath. "I can't go on much farther. Let's turn around. I'm going home."

Only turning her head long enough to see her friend slow her scooter to a crawl, Iris shook her head and continued with her journey. She wasn't going to give up now. With each expanse that passed, her curiosity grew greater and greater.

While it was normal to see buggies traveling across the country to visit others within the community, Jason was heading toward an area that was unfamiliar to Iris. To the best of her knowledge, there were no Amish who even lived in these parts.

Pushing herself forward, Iris ignored the pain in her aching legs as she battled to continue trying to catch up.

In the distance, she could see Jason turn his buggy off the road and pull into the parking lot of a small, unfamiliar building. In the growing darkness, Iris could see bright lights shine forth from the building. Raucous music rang out into the emptiness of the countryside.

Making her way closer to the building, Iris slowed her speed so she would be less noticeable.

If she was worried about being seen, she had no reason to fear. The closer she got to the building, the more obvious it became that Jason was not on the look-out for any other Amish – his attentions were elsewhere.

He jumped down from the buggy and turned only long enough to sling his black jacket onto the seat. Iris let out a gasp of surprise when she saw in the bright light of the building that Jason was no longer dressed in his Amish attire but was instead wearing a pair of blue jeans and a sleeveless T-shirt.

Leading her scooter toward a shadowy area around the back of the building, she leaned it against the wall. Then she caught sight of a window and crept toward it. Standing on tiptoe, she peered into the smoky room through the glass.

Iris felt her heart catch in her throat when she recognized what it was.

"A *bar*," she exclaimed as if somehow speaking it aloud would awaken her from her confusion. What was Jason doing at a bar? Iris had never known him to drink. Of course, in all honesty, Iris didn't really know much about him at all. During their time together, she had been more interested in keeping him as a boyfriend rather than actually getting to know him.

Staring into the building, Iris's eyes traveled through the groups of people surrounding the counter. Several scantily clad women were leaning against the bar, chatting with an older man. They were obviously trying to show off their tanned legs in their short shorts.

Catching sight of Jason as he sauntered through the crowd, Iris felt like she might be sick. He walked directly toward the counter, pushing his way between the older man and the poorly-dressed women.

Ordering and receiving a drink, Jason held it to his lips and downed it all in one gulp. It seemed that this wasn't the first time he'd enjoyed some alcoholic beverages.

After getting a second drink, Jason began to pay attention to one of the girls. Iris watched in horror as they not only laughed together, but he also began to put his hands on her bare arms and her back. Iris wished she could hear what they were saying; although, in all honesty, she wasn't sure she wanted to know.

Jason pulled himself off his stool to his feet and grabbed the woman by the arm, leading her across the hardwood floor to an area where couples were dancing. Putting his arms around her, he let his hands trail across her almost naked back as he snuggled up against her and began to guide her across the floor.

Tears gathered in Iris's eyes as the reality hit her: She, Iris, was *not* the only girl in Jason's life.

After the song finished, Jason went back to the bar for another drink and then reached for the woman's friend. Taking her in his arms, he began to dance with her as well, going so far as to even lean in for a kiss.

Hot tears filled Iris's eyes. How could she have been so stupid? How could she have believed that anyone cared about her? Obviously, Jason had only been spending time with her because he felt sorry for her. Just like everyone else, he also believed Iris was ugly and not enough.

Reaching up to wipe at her eyes, Iris realized she couldn't stand to watch the scene unfold before her any longer. Grabbing for her scooter, she hopped back on and started toward the road.

Chapter Six

Riding in the darkness was difficult and with every turn of her wheels, Iris felt like her heart was breaking a little more.

"Why?" she cried out into the stillness of the night. "Why is this happening? Why am I such an ugly, disgusting person that no one wants me?"

Squinting around the tears in her eyes, Iris didn't see the pothole in the road. Before she knew what was happening, she had sailed over the handle bars of her scooter and landed hard against the pavement.

Now, her emotional pain was compounded by the pain of her injuries. Her ankle felt like it was twisted, and in the streetlamp, she saw blood gathering on her knee.

Forcing herself back to her feet, she grabbed for her scooter, hoping she could manage to hobble home. It was getting late, and her parents were sure to wonder what had happened to her. She didn't know for how long she'd stumbled along before she heard the familiar clip-clop of a buggy gaining on her. She didn't even have to turn around to realize who it surely was – Jason.

At that moment, Iris couldn't stand to see him. She forced herself onto the scooter but winced in pain as she tried to maneuver it.

The sound of the buggy approaching grew louder by the second.

For a moment, Iris hoped she could find a place to hide, but it was too late.

"Iris." Jason's voice called out, his tone slurred. Pulling his horses to a crawl, he repeated, "Iris...is that you?"

Iris took the only course of action she knew – she grabbed her scooter and hobbled toward the side of the road, hoping to hide in the tall grass.

"Iris!" Jason had pulled his buggy to a stop now. Stumbling down from the seat, he shone a headlamp in Iris's direction as he exclaimed, "Iris, what's going on? Why are you out here?"

Recognizing she needed someone to take her home, Iris shook her head and forced herself to explain. "I was out riding my scooter, and it got late...I had a spill and hurt my ankle."

Jason came close and reached for her scooter and picked it up, putting it into the back of his buggy. Then, he took Iris by the hand and helped her up onto the seat.

"Come on," he muttered as he let his hands trail across her back. "Come on with me. I'll take you home."

But when Jason climbed up onto the buggy seat beside Iris, it seemed that driving his horse was the last thing on his mind. He scooted his body closer to hers, filling her senses with the smell of alcohol.

"Iris, Iris, Iris," he muttered with a laugh as he leaned over to give her a kiss. "You really are a trouble-maker, aren't you?"

Jason often had a way of making Iris feel uncomfortable, but tonight was even worse than usual. Sucking in a deep breath, she wished she could magically transport herself home. She wished she had taken Lydia's advice and never followed Jason's buggy in the first place.

"Please, Jason," Iris begged as tears threatened to once again overtake her. "My ankle hurts so badly. I just want to get home."

"Home, home, home," Jason's voice slurred, and he chuckled. Grabbing the reigns tighter in his hands, he loudly announced, "Then we'll get home."

With a cluck of his tongue, he urged the horse forward, forcing it to go faster and faster.

Jason's wild driving had scared Iris before, but now he seemed completely out of control. She found her head swimming as the buggy jostled down the road, the horse panting with the exertion.

"Stop Jason!" Iris screamed, unable to hold in her fear any longer. He was drunk and not thinking clearly, and she reached across him to grab for the reins.

"Slow down, Beauty!" she called out to the horse, easing the buggy down to a slower pace.

The dark horse was breathing heavily, as if glad for a chance to catch her breath.

"Hey," Jason snarled, his face twisted into a scowl in the light of the moon. "What do you think you're doing?"

Iris was so frustrated and upset, she hardly cared what he said or did. Jutting out her chin, she exclaimed, "I want to slow down. For goodness sake, Jason, you're drunk and you're going to get us both killed."

Nodding his head, Jason mumbled, "Maybe you're right. I am drunk." Taking the reins back from her, he slowed the horse even more before looking at Iris and whispering, "But I know why you slowed the buggy. You slowed it down so we could do this..."

Before Iris even knew what he was doing, Jason had yanked her into his arms, pressed his body against hers and began to kiss her with sloppy urgency.

Iris struggled to break free from his grasp, but Jason held on tighter.

"Hey," he exclaimed, his breath hot and stale against her face. "How about we do something more tonight? How about we get even closer? How about..."

He began to clumsily work with her prayer *kapp*, trying to wrench it off her head.

Realizing where his attentions were going and feeling panicked for a way to escape, Iris slapped him right against the face, her palm stinging with the impact of the blow.

Jason's eyes got large and his mouth dropped open. For a moment, Iris was almost frightened he might hit her back.

"Get out of my buggy!" he snapped, his voice sounding more frightening than Iris could have expected. "Get out of my buggy. You can walk."

Iris hurried to obey his command, anxious to put as much distance between them as possible.

Jason got out, grabbed her scooter, and threw it out of the buggy, sending it landing onto the asphalt with a crash.

"You're not worth it, Iris," Jason informed her sternly, his gaze steely as he glared at her in the light of his headlamps. "Believe me, I know you're not. No matter what you do, you'd never be worth my time." Pausing for effect, he added, "Your brothers are right, you're not only ugly, but you're also a waste of time."

Climbing back into the buggy and grabbing the reins, his urged his horse forward, leaving Iris standing alongside the road with her scooter at her feet.

By the time Iris hobbled back home, everyone was sound asleep with all the lanterns in the house completely extinguished.

She limped to her room where she poured some water into a basin and worked to soothe her poor ankle. She was so exhausted she hardly realized that sobs were overtaking her until the tears poured down her cheeks.

"I am ugly," Iris whispered into the stillness of her room. "I am ugly and unwanted, and that will never change. I was a fool to think it could."

The reality of her fate hit Iris full force. No matter what she did, she would never be enough for a man. She had tried so hard to keep Jason's attention, but he had still run off to dance at a bar with those women.

Remembering all she had done in an attempt to keep Jason as a beau, Iris felt a deep surge of embarrassment and shame. She had given so much to him, and yet it still wasn't enough.

He was right...she wasn't worth his time.

Chapter Seven

Henry Rupp drew in a deep breath of the hot summer air as he bent over one of the tomato plants and gently worked to tie it to a stake. This one plant in particular had a rough time of it, starting out smaller than the rest of the tomatoes and then being trampled by an escaped cow who managed to make her way through their garden.

"You never have been one to give up, have you?" Henry's dad commented as he walked up behind Henry and gave his son a friendly slap on the back. "No matter what, you've always been there to care of the sick or the hurting." Smiling, he added, "I would have simply let that tomato plant go."

Henry only shrugged and straightened his back. "Every living thing is worth trying to save."

As the words tumbled over Henry's lips, he thought of Iris

Glick. He worried about her more than he wanted to admit, even to himself. The stories Jason spread about her were so hard to imagine, and yet Henry feared there might be some truth to them. Iris had never had a beau, and it seemed she was willing to do whatever it took to keep Jason now that she had him.

"You know," Henry's dad spoke up, "The bishop talked to me about the need for someone to organize some youth volleyball games to help include some of the new Amish kids who have moved into the community."

Shaking his head, his father added, "I'm afraid that some of them are having a hard time fitting in. You know the trouble kids can get into when they feel like outcasts...too many times, they choose to leave the Amish faith behind and instead chase what the world has to offer in hopes it will provide them with excitement."

He finished by saying, "So many times, those who leave, get involved in alcohol or drugs or women and their lives completely fall apart."

Or they get involved with bad boys, Henry thought to himself, his mind traveling back again to Iris and her relationship with Jason Rutger.

"I was thinking you might be interested in working to organize these volleyball games," Henry's dad said. "In fact, I told the bishop I'd talk with you about it."

Shrugging, Henry wiped some sweat from his brow and nodded his head. "*Jah*, I guess I could do that."

At this moment, it was hard for him to think of anything other than his concerns about Iris.

"You'll need some help," his dad continued as he scooted his boot over the soft garden dirt. "But I think you can find someone easily enough. Perhaps Iris Glick would like to work with you."

The name took Henry by such surprise that he felt sure his dad might see his instant discomfort. Forcing himself to remain calm, he nonchalantly shrugged and replied, "Maybe so…if her beau doesn't mind."

"It's just a thought." Standing up straighter, his dad gave his beard a tug before looking up at the sky and announcing, "I'd better go get those cows fed before it starts raining."

With that, he turned and left Henry alone with his thoughts. Breathing deeply, Henry considered his father's suggestion. Could he really find the courage to ask Iris to help him? The thought of risking rejection once again was almost more than he could stomach. Besides, if she was already so firmly involved with Jason, she probably didn't have the time or the inclination to think about helping him with a volleyball game.

No, as far as Henry could tell, Iris Glick was out of his reach.

Standing over the wash basin, Iris worked to remove some dried barbecue sauce that was stuck to one of the plates. As she worked, she was in a constant battle to keep her emotions in check. All day, thoughts of Jason played through her mind, and his words seemed to repeat themselves over and over again.

"Hey, you," Ezekiel exclaimed as he walked past her and gave her a less-than-friendly shove on her back. "When are you going to be done in here? I want to get washed up before I see Rhoda tonight, and you're hogging up the space."

Rhoda Schmidt was a girl who had just moved to the community. For some reason, she seemed to be interested in Ezekiel, with the two of them frequently going out on buggy rides together.

Just the thought of Iris's older brother having a steady girlfriend made Iris's heart ache. Ezekiel was a cruel, annoying, boorish boy. If anyone in the world deserved to be left alone, it was him. And yet, he was able to attract dates while Iris couldn't keep the attention of a boy no matter how many boundaries she crossed or what she was willing to do.

"There," she muttered as she set the last dish aside. "I'm done."

"Bout time, slow poke," Ezekiel shot out another insult with a shake of his head.

A knock on the back door gave Iris an excuse to leave the

room without another word. She knew it was useless to try and stand up against her brother and today, she felt weaker than usual and didn't even try.

Making her way to the door, she pulled it open to reveal her friend, Lydia, standing on the back porch.

Lydia gave Iris a secretive smile before looking over her shoulder, obviously checking to see who was around before she started to talk.

"Iris," Lydia said in little more than a whisper. "Can you talk?"

Talking was the last thing Iris wanted to do. Just the idea of trying to explain what had happened the night before was more than she could bear. But this was Lydia. And Lydia would expect to hear what had happened. Motioning outside, Iris suggested, "Let's go out there to chat."

Once the girls were both on the back porch, Iris closed the house door behind her, anxious to be away from the prying ears of her brothers.

"Tell me what happened last night," Lydia said, her words rushing out like a flood when she was alone with Iris. "Where did Jason end up going? Did you follow him all the way?"

Iris leaned her back against the bench and shook her head slowly. Closing her eyes, she blew out her breath in a sigh. "Lydia, I don't think I want to talk about this right now."

Lydia put a hand on her friend's arm. "But did you see him? Did you argue? Was he really going to work?"

Realizing there was no way to stop Lydia's torrent of questions until she gave in and answered, Iris forced out the fastest explanation that she could muster. "He went to a bar, Lydia. He went to a bar where he danced with *Englisch* women and even kissed them."

Lydia's eyes got huge, her disbelief only making Iris feel worse. "He *kissed* them?" Lydia cried, as if it was something too horrible for her to even fathom. "Then what happened? Did you confront him? Does he know that you saw?"

Reaching up to wipe at her eyes, Iris admitted, "I don't know what he thinks I saw at the bar, but we did meet each other. He found me on the road and tried to give me a ride home...it was terrible. Just terrible."

Memories of Jason pawing at her, trying to get so much more than she was willing to give plagued Iris, and she thought she might be sick. Shaking her head, she said, "I don't want to talk about what happened between us. Just know that Jason and I are over."

Something akin to mixed relief and disgust crossed Lydia's face as she vehemently declared, "Well, *gut*. It's high time you let that scummy boy go. I knew he was bad news all along, but now...well, now I'm totally convinced. He isn't *gut* enough to even shine your shoes."

Lydia's words did little to make Iris feel better. No matter what her friend said, deep in her heart, Iris knew the truth. The problem wasn't with Jason – the problem was with her. She was worthless. Jason might be a cad, but he only proved it was impossible for Iris to find anyone who would love her.

"Just be glad he's gone." Lydia exclaimed, crossing her arms over her chest as she boldly declared, "The next time I see him, I'm not even going to pretend to be civil."

Iris couldn't stand listening to her friend any longer. Shaking her head, she felt angry at Lydia as she exclaimed, "I don't want to hear about this right now, Lydia. I told you that I didn't want to talk about it. I just ... can't."

Lydia opened her mouth and then closed it as if she thought better of what she was about to say. Finally, she threw up her hands and shook her head. "Fine. I'm sorry. I'll leave you alone now." Turning, she headed back toward her scooter.

Iris watched as Lydia maneuvered her scooter drive and back toward the country road.

The pain that Iris felt in her heart only seemed to intensify by the moment. A hot sob started to rise in her throat, and she wondered how she could possibly endure the heartache she was feeling. She was so angry at Jason and the way he had betrayed her, but she was just as angry – if not more so – with herself. How could she have given away so much of herself in an effort to keep him? But even as she scolded herself, she knew she would do the same things all over again if it meant receiving attention from a handsome young man.

Or would she?

Had it been worth it? Truly?

For a few weeks, Jason Rutger had made her feel important enough to be pursued. She had cherished the feeling and yearned to feel that way again.

Looking up at the dark clouds gathering in the sky, Iris decided to head to the garden and dig out some of the weeds before the clouds gave way to rain. Grabbing for the hoe that was resting against the side of the house, Iris went out to the garden. She savored the feel of the loose dirt between her bare toes as she removed the pesky weeds from between the veggies. As she worked, she poured some of her frustration and pain into her effort. Soft raindrops hit her cheeks, blending in with the tears that were now dripping from her eyes.

"What is wrong with me?" Iris asked aloud, allowing her frustration voice, "What is wrong with me?"

Lowering her hoe, she looked up to the sky and whispered, "*Gott*...why did you make me so unappealing?"

It felt like she was simply speaking to herself. Obviously, even God himself had turned his back on her.

Lifting the hoe again, she brought it down with a vengeance

on a nearby weed, digging at it with all her might. Jerking the hoe back, Iris realized she had stuck one of the bush bean plants in her tirade. The little plant had been chopped to bits; its life snuffed out before it could even start to provide food.

Something about seeing what she had done to the bean plant sent Iris over the edge. She dropped to her knees in the dirt and grabbed for the pieces of leaves and vine, tears streaming down her cheeks as she tried to somehow restore the broken plant.

"Poor thing," Iris exclaimed with a shake of her head. "Poor little plant...what have I done to you?"

What are you doing to yourself?

Iris heard the voice clearly in her mind.

You care so much about a bean plant that will be gone within a season...and yet you don't care about yourself, a person Gott made and fashioned for eternity.

Iris looked up, as if she expected to see someone. But she was all alone.

The raindrops increased in intensity, soaking her from her prayer *kapp* down to her dark blue dress.

It was true. Iris was made by God, fashioned by His own hands, created for a purpose. She had heard this lesson her entire life and yet, somehow, the truth of it had never really entered her heart. Iris had grown up so consumed by her own plain appearance, she didn't grasp that she was actually someone designed and loved by an all-powerful Creator.

She cared more about a bean plant than she cared about herself.

The reality of it all hit Iris with full force. When she had been compromising her standards with Jason as if she were worthless, God had always loved her and had seen her as someone precious. He had loved her so much that he had sent Christ to die for her on the cross, just so Iris could be with him for eternity. And yet she had treated herself as if she were of less importance than a bean plant.

"I am sorry, Lord *Gott*," she whispered as the dirt around her knees became mud from the rain. "I'm so sorry for not seeing myself as someone you love...someone you created. I am sorry I've acted as if my life wasn't enough, when you made me to be exactly as you want. *Gott,* please show me a new way of life. I'm ready to start living differently."

Chapter Eight

Lying in her bed that afternoon, Iris listened absentmindedly to the rain that was still pattering on the roof. She felt exhausted, and yet at the same time, exhilarated. After rushing to finish her chores, she appreciated the opportunity to get off by herself where she could consider all the things God had revealed to her that day.

A tap on her bedroom door gave her a start, and she could only hope it wasn't one of her brothers ready to test her new-found faith in herself.

"Iris?" It was the voice of her mother calling through the thick wooden door. "Iris, it's *Mamm*. I just wanted to let you know that there's a buggy parked at the end of our lane. It looks like Jason Rutger. I don't know why he's not coming to the house. Were you expecting him?"

Jason? He was *there?*

Iris's heart instantly leapt in her chest. What was Jason doing back? Was it possible he was ready to apologize for his actions the previous night and take steps to restore their relationship?

Even as the thought crossed her mind, Iris pushed it aside. Sucking in a deep breath, she steeled herself to do what she knew was right. No matter how much she might miss having the attention of a boy, she now realized she didn't need a boyfriend to prove anything or make her valuable – those were things the Lord had already done.

Iris called out, "Thanks, *Mamm*, but I'm not expecting Jason. If he wants to talk, I suppose he can come up here to the house."

Mrs. Glick made a noise that sounded like she agreed before Iris heard her footsteps retreating back down the hall.

Leaning against the headboard of her bed, Iris closed her eyes and breathed in the freedom that came from turning Jason away. It was time for her to embrace what the Lord had planned for her life and to stop using Jason to fill a void that only God could truly touch.

The next day, Iris had just put a fresh loaf of bread into the oven when she heard a buggy pull into their drive.

Her entire family had left to go visit a neighbor and share a meal; however, Iris had opted to stay behind. The good feeling that had invaded her heart in the garden was still there that morning, and she relished the idea of being alone to work through her thoughts.

Letting out a sigh, she tried to hide her disappointment at realizing that her family had returned so soon.

She'd enjoyed the afternoon working around the house alone and spending time in prayer. She'd hoped to have several more hours to think about what the Lord was doing in her life, but it looked like her solitude was over.

A rap against the front door assured Iris it wasn't her family that had returned.

"Who on earth?" she wondered aloud as she wiped her floury hands against her apron before making her way to the door.

Swinging the front door open, Iris found the dejected form of Jason Rutger standing on her doorstep. With his felt hat held in his hands, he looked more somber than she had ever seen him look. He glanced down at his feet, evidently too ashamed to even meet Iris's gaze.

"Iris," he muttered as he darted a glance up at her, "when I met your family on the road earlier, I was hoping I'd be able to find you here alone."

Putting a hand on her hip, Iris raised an eyebrow and thought about shutting the door without even hearing him out.

"What does that have to do with anything?" she asked, her voice snappier than she intended, "Why does it matter if my family is here or not. We have nothing we need to talk about in private. After the other night, I don't even want to see you, let alone be with you."

Putting his hand against the door so she couldn't shut it without giving him a chance to speak his piece, Jason looked at her with blue eyes that were filled with remorse.

"Iris," he tried again. "I know things went a little bad with us the other night..." Noticing her expression, he shrugged and went on, "Okay, very bad with us. I'd been drinking, and it made me do things I wouldn't normally do. Honestly, you know that's the truth. You know I don't act like that when I'm sober. It's just...well, sometimes the urge to go out and party overtakes me. I'm trying to do better, honestly, I am." He reached for Iris's hand, but she jerked it away.

"Iris, listen. I'm so sorry about everything that happened. I'm sorry about anything I said to hurt you. I really can't even remember everything from that night. It's like I was a different person. I swear to you, I will never do that again."

Crossing her arms over her chest, Iris narrowed her eyes. "You're right, Jason, you will never do it again. You'll never even have the opportunity to do it again because I'm not going anywhere else with you." Shaking her head, she almost laughed at the freedom that filled her.

She continued, "Jason, the only reason you ever went out with me was because you saw me as someone you could control and manipulate. You never actually liked me as a person. And, truth be told, I never liked you much, either. You were just someone who I needed to make me feel better about myself. And I'm sorry about that. It was wrong of me."

"That can't be true," Jason protested. "Iris, we have true feelings for each other. Surely you have experienced them."

For the first time, Iris felt sorry for Jason as she watched him falter, trying his best to win her back. But, try as hard as he might, Iris wasn't going there again. She looked at him squarely.

"Something changed the other night. Well, it started changing then, but it really changed yesterday. *Gott* has opened my eyes to something I never realized before." Squaring her shoulders, she boldly declared, "I'm valuable and I'm worthwhile, no matter what you may say. I don't need you or anyone else to make me feel better about myself."

"Iris..." Jason continued, his voice pleading. "Don't say that. I always thought well of you. I did."

Iris shook her head. "Nee, Jason, that's not true. And I would sooner be single for the rest of my life than go out with you again."

Taken by total surprise at her statement, Jason stepped back, giving Iris the perfect opportunity to shut the door, securely barring him from the house and away from her completely.

Leaning against the back of the door, Iris shook her head in awe as she considered what had just happened. A few weeks ago, she would have done anything to re-gain Jason's approval – and now she was shutting him completely out of her life.

It felt good to realize she didn't have to grovel to a man or let him misuse her to be of some value. God had given Iris her value, and she could only hope she would continue to appreciate that truth more with each day.

"Please, *Gott*," she whispered into the stillness of the room, "never let me forget."

Iris spent the rest of her day working around the house, basking in her newfound freedom and appreciation for herself. By the time her family got home, Iris felt like she was floating on a cloud.

She continued to spend her evening baking and was taking some sticky rolls out of the oven when Ezekiel came and plopped himself down at the kitchen table.

Steeling her nerves for what was about to come, Iris could only pray silently for strength to endure any tormenting her brother would dish out. While Iris had a new respect and appreciation for herself, she was still very tender, and it would be easy for her confidence to melt.

"Hey, Droopy Eyes," Ezekiel barked, his voice sounding like an army commander. "Hand me one of those rolls."

Ignoring him completely, Iris worked to ice the rolls with the frosting she'd just made.

"Hey, you," Ezekiel tried again. "Are you deaf? I asked you for one of those rolls."

Turning slowly, Iris took every ounce of strength she could gather to look at her brother. Staring at him coolly, she watched as his confidence faltered the longer her gaze stayed on him.

"Ezekiel," she spoke finally, her voice coming out in a controlled, methodical manner, "you have spent my entire life demeaning me and calling me mean things. This is where it stops. From now on, I will only answer to my name."

Her brother's jaw dropped, and he stared at her in open disbelief. There was something very rewarding about seeing him squirm and look uncomfortable in her presence.

Deciding to add a finishing touch to her speech, she announced, "You no longer have any power over me, brother. I forgive you. Now, if you'd like to ask for one of these sticky rolls in a respectful manner and using my given name, I'll be happy to give you one."

Ezekiel stared at her and then shook his head, his surprise replaced by disgust. Jumping to his feet, Iris heard him mumble something about "not putting up with this" before he sauntered out of the room, clearly eager to escape.

Although Iris could have hoped for a better response to her announcement, her first attempt to put Ezekiel in his place was worth it.

Picking up one of the gooey rolls, Iris smiled to herself as she took a big bite, enjoying the taste of the sugar on her tongue, along with the satisfaction of knowing her brother would never again have such power over her.

Chapter Nine

Sunday night, Iris called a paid driver to take her to the singing. While her parents insisted it was ridiculous that she wouldn't travel in the buggy with her brothers, Iris was more than happy to take some of the egg money she had saved and pay her own way to the event. While Ezekiel and Thomas had both treated her with more respect over the last few days, she saw no need to put herself in a position where she couldn't escape them.

Going to the singing at all seemed risky. Iris dreaded the idea of seeing Jason Rutger again and was afraid he might try to talk to her. Sitting in the backseat of the driver's car, Iris took shaky breaths as she considered what she would do if Jason made a scene.

Closing her eyes, old feelings of uncertainty and powerlessness overwhelmed her.

"Please, *Gott*," she whispered a prayer softly, "Help me to get through this."

Iris had considered simply staying home from the singing entirely but had ultimately decided pushing herself forward was the best idea. If she were to hide from her problems, it would only make them worse. She needed to face Jason head-on and find her place among the Amish young folk.

When she arrived at the Bontragers' home, buggies were already flooding the yard – proof that plenty of youth were going to be there for the sing.

Getting out of her driver's car, Iris told him what time to pick her up before making her way through the throngs of teens gathered on the Bontragers' lawn. The boys were laughing together while some of the girls stood aside to giggle and whisper secrets.

Iris was seeing them all through new eyes. She had spent her entire life feeling like an outsider who didn't really fit in with the others. But now, everything was different.

"Hello, Iris," one of the girls called out, a broad smile across her cheerful face.

"Hello, Suzy," Iris returned with a smile of her own.

For the first time, Iris noticed Suzy's smile was a tad bit crooked, and her front teeth stuck out a bit; however, it seemed Suzy wasn't at all concerned with how her teeth looked. Instead, she was smiling and showing the warmth of her kind heart.

"Hello, Gladys." Iris nodded her head toward another girl.

Gladys was considered one of the prettiest girls in the community with her soft brown eyes and curly dark hair. For as long as Iris had known her, Gladys had struggled with skin conditions that sometimes gave her a rash. Despite this, Gladys always came to the singings and no one treated her any differently.

Look at me. Iris thought, *what a foolish girl I've been. While the other girls have been able to enjoy life in spite of their imperfections, I've let mine dictate everything. If these girls can be happy with the way Gott made them, doesn't it only make sense that I can do the same?*

Iris's newfound confidence was magnified as she made her way toward the Bontragers' house, eager to find Lydia and make up with her after their spat during the week. She found her inside.

"Iris," Lydia looked at her tentatively when she approached. Iris could see the apprehension in Lydia's eyes and hated that she had been so harsh with her dear friend.

"Lydia," Iris returned, stepping up to her friend's side. "I'm sorry for blowing up at you the other day..."

"*Nee*," Lydia was shaking her head. "You shouldn't be sorry. I'm the one who is sorry. I knew you were going through a rough time, and I pushed you too hard."

Looking around the Bontragers' kitchen to see who might be within listening distance, Iris lowered her voice to ask, "Do you know where Jason is?"

Lydia's eyes widened, and she shook her head slowly, "*Ach*, Iris, I thought you might have heard by now... Last night he got in trouble with the law for being drunk and disorderly. He's still in an *Englisch* jail. His parents are terribly upset, but they say they're going to leave him in there until his court date."

A mixture of shock and sympathy washed over Iris. She was glad she wouldn't have to encounter the young man who had done so much to hurt her, and yet, she also regretted that Jason had let himself go so far.

Looking down, Iris considered the ways she had tried to use Jason to fill a hole in her heart. Obviously, he was battling with a host of his own problems. She could only hope that eventually, he would find the same peace she was now experiencing.

"Are you all right?" Lydia whispered, her voice sounding uncertain. "Maybe I shouldn't have told you about Jason. I didn't know if you'd care or not."

Looking up to meet her friend's eyes, Iris smiled boldly and nodded her head. "*Jah*, Lydia, I'm fine." Reaching out to take Lydia's hands in her own, she couldn't stop from beaming as she said, "So much has changed in my life. It's a long story and a lot to explain, but *Gott* has worked a miracle since you left my house the other day." Motioning toward an empty bench in the corner of the room, she said, "How about we sit down, and I'll tell you all about it before the singing gets started?"

Standing at the edge of the kitchen, Henry felt unnerved as he stood in the shadows and watched Iris and Lydia chatting together on a bench. They seemed completely oblivious to the rest of the world.

Henry had been afraid Iris wouldn't show up to the singing when her brothers arrived without her riding in their buggy. He had already heard that Jason Rutger had gotten in some kind of trouble with the law, and Henry was afraid Iris would be either too ashamed or too sad to show her face among them.

But Henry's fears had been proven unfounded. Iris had arrived at the youth gathering and seemed more outgoing and happier than ever.

Watching her smile boldly as she repeated something to her friend, Henry cocked his head to one side and tried to imagine just what might have made such a change in her. All he knew was that she certainly didn't seem like the same Iris from even a few short days ago.

Henry was overcome with a desire to go to her side and bluntly ask what had happened, but he worked to keep himself in check.

"Steady, Henry," he whispered to himself. "Hold on until later. This isn't the time."

The kitchen door opened, and a flood of youth poured into the kitchen, eager to get started with their evening events. Henry went with them to the large table that had been set up for the singing, allowing himself to get caught up in the activities and forcing his thoughts away from Iris.

Sitting at the far end of the table with Lydia by herself, Iris felt like she could sing louder than ever before. The music practically poured out of her heart. She had never been so light-hearted or happy in her life.

Iris now felt free to simply enjoy her life without comparing herself to all the other girls. Glancing down the table, her gaze landed on Henry Rupp. He was openly watching her, studying her with a look of something almost like confusion.

As soon as Iris looked at him, he quickly averted his eyes, his cheeks growing somewhat red as if he had been caught doing something he shouldn't.

What was Henry Rupp doing looking at her? What was he thinking? Was he noticing her nose? As soon as the thought crossed her mind, she hastened to push it aside. She wasn't going to allow herself to get hung up on her appearance ever again.

A nudge to her elbow made Iris jump, and she turned to look into the knowing face of Lydia. "Looks like you've caught the eye of somebody," she whispered as she leaned in close.

Her words made Iris instantly blush. What was her friend implying? Iris had always thought Henry was a fine young man, but she'd never considered the fact that he might give her a second glance. He was always kind to her, but Iris had simply taken his kindness as sympathy.

"Lydia," Iris whispered, darting her gaze around the room as she tried to determine who might have heard her friend's bold suggestion. "Hush. You know Henry doesn't think of me like that."

"I wouldn't be so sure," Lydia replied with a teasing grin. "I've noticed him looking at you in the past."

Although Iris felt a hint of excitement at the prospect of Henry giving her attention, she also found herself overwhelmed with embarrassment. Looking down at her hands, she could only hope the other youth around her didn't notice how unsettled she was.

Chapter Ten

Although Iris had a wonderful time at the singing, she was actually glad when it was over. The last week had been an exhilarating and yet exhausting experience, leaving her tired and ready to get home to her bed. As the young folk began to gather their belongings and head off to ride home in their buggies, Iris pulled herself to her feet.

"It was *gut* to see you, Lydia," she said with a heart-felt smile as she reached out and gave her friend a quick hug.

"Good to see you, too, Iris," Lydia smiled, her face practically beaming. "It's so nice to see you happy again. I don't actually think I've ever seen you look any better."

A pat on the shoulder made Iris jump and turn around in surprise. Her jaw dropped open when she realized that Henry Rupp was standing right behind her.

Henry put his hands in his pockets and weaved back and forth, squinting and coughing nervously before he said, "I've got something I need to ask you, Iris."

Feeling her breath catch in her throat, Iris swallowed hard. "What would that be?"

"Well," Henry began slowly, "the Bishop is talking about organizing some youth volleyball games. He wants to get some of the new youth involved in the community and help them to feel more included." Looking at Iris, he squinted one eye as he asked, "I need someone to help the girls. I don't suppose you'd be willing to consider helping, would you?"

Iris's heart leapt in her chest. Help out with some of the awkward youth in their community? Iris had never been offered such an appealing task in her life. She relished the thought of helping some of the youth who, like she had, felt like outcasts and unappreciated.

"That is...if your boyfriend wouldn't mind," Henry hurried to add, his face blushing as if he were embarrassed by the entire situation.

Iris battled her own sense of embarrassment as she admitted, "Jason and I...well, we're not...things went sour between us. We're not courting anymore."

It would have been hard not to notice the look of relief that crossed Henry's face. Raising his eyebrows, he said, "That's great news. I mean—" he hurried to correct himself. "It's not great that things didn't work out, but it's great that you'll be able to help. I'm sorry that you and Jason...I mean, I'm sorry that you got hurt...if you did get hurt, that is."

Iris had never seen a boy more awkward and unable to speak. Something about watching him was surprisingly sweet.

Giving a shrug, Iris smiled. "It's okay. I think Jason and I weren't meant to be."

A beeping of a horn outside alerted Iris her driver had arrived. Giving Henry another smile, she said, "Well, that would be my driver. I guess I'd better go."

"See you, Iris," Henry called out after her as she started for the front door. "I'll be in contact so we can make plans about the volleyball."

Stepping out onto the stone path that led to her waiting ride, Iris's brows knit together in confusion when she saw that her driver, Ben Johnson, was standing outside the vehicle with the hood up in the air. He was running one hand through his hair and letting out annoyed noises as he looked down into the engine.

"I've got bad news, Miss Glick," he said with a grunt as he motioned toward the smoke that was curling from the car. "Something has happened, and my car has overheated. I called my son, and he's on the way to check it out with me.

But it could be another hour before he can get here. Do you mind waiting? Or is there some way that you could ride home with one of your brothers?"

The thought of having to catch a ride home with either Ezekiel or Thomas made Iris feel dismay; however, she had no option but to think of it as the Lord's will. Was God testing her ability to remain confident in her new beliefs about herself?

Sucking in a deep breath, Iris nodded her head and assured her driver. "It's fine, Mr. Johnson. I'm sure I can find a ride home. You just worry about taking care of yourself and getting your car fixed. I'm sorry this happened."

Ben Johnson was already studying his engine again, clearly oblivious to everything she was saying.

Turning, Iris braced herself to find one of her brothers and ask for a ride in their buggy. But before she had a chance to look for either Ezekiel or Thomas, Iris found herself running right into Henry Rupp.

"*Ach.*" Iris exclaimed. "I'm so sorry. I didn't see you there..."

"It's fine," Henry assured her as he took a step backwards. "I was the one getting up close to eavesdrop. I heard what happened with Mr. Johnson's car." Pausing for a moment, Henry had to gather his courage before he asked, "Would you want me to give you a ride home?"

Iris felt her heart lurch. Could this be happening? Could it be that God had actually used Mr. Johnson's bad fortune to work something so happy in Iris's favor?

Nodding her head almost too vigorously, Iris blushed when she realized how quickly she had accepted his offer. "*Jah*, that would be wonderful *gut*. Thank you so much, Henry."

Sitting on the seat of his buggy with Iris Glick at his side, Henry could hardly believe his night had turned out this way. When he had been uncertain about inviting Iris to help him with the upcoming volleyball games, he'd known it was the right thing to do. Now, he was doubly glad he had found the courage to step forward and ask her. After so many years of rejection, Iris had finally accepted Henry's offer of friendship.

"I can't thank you enough for the ride," Iris spoke up to say, breaking the silence between them.

Gripping the reins tighter in his hands, Henry tried to find something to say in reply. How could he tell her he was more than happy to take her back home to her parents' house? How could he tell her he had always wanted to be closer to her? Surely everything he could say would be coming entirely too soon since she and Jason just broke off their relationship.

Choosing to veer in a different direction, Henry cocked his head to one side and said, "I can see something different about you tonight, Iris. You act...different. Honestly, you even look different."

"*Ach*," Iris said, shifting on the wooden bench beside Henry. "A *gut* kind of different or a bad kind of different?"

"*Gut*," Henry replied before realizing his mistake and hurrying to correct it. "I mean, not that you ever looked bad in any way...but now you just seem...well, so much happier."

Turning to glance at her more directly, Henry could only hope his face wasn't as red as it felt.

To his relief, Iris was smiling pleasantly as she studied his expression. Leaning back against the seat, she let out a contented sigh. "Well, Henry Rupp, that would be quite a story."

Smiling back at her, Henry replied, "I'm always up for a *gut* story."

For the first time in her life, Iris began to open her heart and pour out the details she had worked so hard to keep buried away. She explained how she had grown up feeling so insignificant and ugly, and how she had turned to Jason to give her a measure of confidence. Then, Iris went on to tell Henry about her experience in the garden when she realized the Lord had made her just the way he wanted her.

"I know it sounds crazy," she said, her eyes twinkling with the excitement of it all. "But I feel closer to the Lord *Gott* now than I ever have in my life. Truth be told, I'm actually thanking Him that he made me a little plainer than I would have wanted, simply because it has helped me learn to appreciate my imperfections and to start relying on *Gott* to give me my value."

As Henry listened to her talk, he was swept away with her enthusiasm and new appreciation for life. They reached the Glick home far too quickly, and Henry wished he could continue to ride with her at his side for hours more to come.

"Well," Iris announced as Henry pulled his buggy to a stop at the end of her drive. "I suppose this is *gut*-bye for now."

Henry nodded his head, "*Jah*, *gut*-bye for now...although don't forget we've got to get together sometime this week and make plans for the volleyball games."

Iris clapped her hands together with excitement and assured him, "I wouldn't miss it."

As Henry watched her scurry down from the buggy seat, he wished they were close enough so that he could give her a soft good-night hug or at least take her hand in his own to press it tenderly.

But that's not for tonight, he assured himself. Although, for the first time in his life, Henry knew it might be a possibility in the future. And that was one thing he had never imagined could be a hope for him and Iris Glick.

He tugged the reins and turned his buggy toward home. It had been a good evening. A very, very good evening indeed.

Epilogue

Standing beside the volleyball net, Iris watched as the girls took turns batting the ball back and forth, using their fists to career it over the net.

Volleyball had always been a favorite among the young people and, between her and Henry, they were working hard to ensure these youth got a good start with the wholesome team sport.

Henry. Just thinking his name brought a smile to Iris's lips. Glancing across the lawn, she could see him working with the boys at a different net.

Ach, but he certainly was a handsome beau. Iris considered herself beyond blessed to be able to call him her own.

Smiling at the thought of it all, Iris considered how she and Henry had gotten together the night Mr. Johnsons' car broke down. Iris had thought it was going to be a bad situation, but instead of being a nuisance, God used it to career her into a new, healthier relationship.

It had almost been a year since the night she shared her first buggy ride with Henry, and the two of them had been officially courting now for more than six months.

Looking back at all the many years Iris had spent feeling alone and unworthy, it now seemed like they were simply a bad dream. God had done so much for her—as soon as she was able to open her heart up to him and accept the good things he had planned for her life.

And Jason? Well, Jason was now a nearly-forgotten memory from her past. After he was released from jail, Iris heard he moved on to a different community where he got into even more trouble. Eventually, a preacher who worked in a jail talked to him, and he eventually changed his life. While Jason had chosen not to return to the Amish faith, he had joined a protestant church and now worked with other troubled youth.

"*Gott* had a plan...even for him," Iris mused to herself, amazed by how the Lord never gave up on people, even when they made terrible mistakes.

Glancing back at the team of girls who were shooting the ball back and forth across the net, laughing together as they tried to keep it from hitting the ground, Iris frowned when she noticed one of the girls step back from the group and retreat toward the shelter of a nearby tree.

While it was fine for the girls to step back and take a break from the game, there was something about this young lady that reminded Iris of herself.

Moving away from the other players, Iris approached the girl, silently praying for the Lord to give her the right words to reach her. Although Iris knew most of the girls in their community, this girl was unfamiliar since her family had just moved to the area. She looked to be about thirteen-years-old and Iris struggled to remember her name.

"Hello," Iris greeted her as she reached her side. "You're off here all by yourself. Are you tired of playing volleyball?"

The girl had sat down on the ground, her knees pulled up under her chin, and she looked up at Iris in surprise.

Giving a shrug, she replied, "I dunno." Motioning toward her chubby middle, she explained, "I'm not as fast as the other girls, and I'm not very good at volleyball. My *daed* told me I'd just slow down the team, and I'm afraid he's right. Maybe playing volleyball isn't the best idea for me."

Iris felt her heart break as she considered the girl's situation. "It's hard for everybody when they're just getting started."

Letting out a deep sigh, the girl went on, "My *daed* says I'm too chunky for my own good, and I know it's true. Sometimes he ... he compares me to a cow." Shaking her head, she finished, "I know I need to lose some weight and he's worried about me, but it's just hard when I've got so much... well, other stuff going on."

Reaching down to twirl a piece of grass between her fingers, she explained, "When my *mamm* died, food was the only thing that could make me happy." Throwing up her hands in frustration, she exclaimed, "I guess I'll just be a worthless fatty for the rest of my life."

Lowering herself to the ground beside the girl, Iris inhaled deeply before she slowly stated, "I know how it feels to think you're worthless."

The girl raised an eyebrow and looked at Iris in surprise. "How would you know? You're so perfect."

Iris had to chuckle at the girl's announcement. She began to share the story of her own struggles with her appearance and how focusing on her flaws had almost destroyed her life. As she shared the way God had showed her the value she possessed, Iris could see a difference sweep across the girl's face.

She clasped her hands together, once again grateful for what had happened in her life.

Thank you, Gott, she thought silently as she comforted the girl. *Thank you for my testimony...and thank you for giving me my worth.*

Which of course, she'd had all along.

The End

Continue Reading...

Thank you for reading **Finding Her Worth! Are you wondering what to read next?** Why not read **Dawn's Discovery. Here's a peek for you:**

Spring had well and truly arrived, Dawn thought to herself as she drove her family's cart down the country lane that led toward the town of Baker's Corner. Amongst the green hedgerows bloomed red maples, setting Indiana alight. Dawn loved this time of year. Although the smell of rain was in the air from an overnight downpour, the sun had risen warm and bright. Winter was officially over, and Dawn felt as though change were on the horizon. *Change.* She needed it.

The past year had been long and hard, and not just for her, but for her entire family. Her sister Debbie's accident last summer had left Debbie unable to do her usual chores around the farm, and Dawn found herself taking up the extra work as well as caring for her sister. Not that she was bitter about it, but she was tired. She didn't think someone her age should have permanent dark marks under her eyes, but they were there, nonetheless, along with a single strands of grey hair that she had plucked out only the day before. *Grey hair.* At twenty. Not that she was vain, but still...

She stocked up the cart at the feed store, stopping to chat awhile with Claire, the smiling young woman who worked there. Dawn liked her trips to the feed store; they meant getting away from the farm for a couple of hours, and she always dragged that time out for as long as possible. Of course, she knew she was needed back home, but she just couldn't make herself hurry too much.

Claire helped her load the sacks of feed onto the cart, and then with a wave, disappeared back inside. Dawn envied her. She had a job outside of home, something Dawn yearned for; she envied the independence Claire seemed to have of a life outside of her family. There was more than a little freedom in that, Dawn thought.

She sighed and climbed back up onto the cart. She took Doris's reins in her hands and urged the grey mare into motion, moving at a decided quick trot. Dawn had just one more errand to run while she was here, and that was to stop by the fabric store for some thread and a few other items.

She left Doris and the cart around the corner and walked the short distance to the fabric store. *Button Up* was owned by Grace Epp, an older Mennonite woman, who was generally liked by just about everyone. She always had a smile for her customers, and today was no different. She greeted Dawn warmly, asking after her and her family's health.

"What are you after today?" Grace asked.

CLICK HERE To Read More:

http://www.ticahousepublishing.com/amish-miller.html

Thank you for Reading

If you **love Amish Romance, Click Here:**

https://amish.subscribemenow.com/

to find out about all **New Hannah Miller Amish Romance Releases!** We will let you know as soon as they become available!

If you enjoyed ***Finding Her Worth!*** would you kindly take a couple minutes to leave a positive review on Amazon? It only takes a moment, and positive reviews truly make a difference. I would be so grateful! Thank you!

Turn the page to discover more Hannah Miller Amish Romances just for you!

More Amish Romance from Hannah Miller

Visit HERE for Hannah Miller's Amish Romance

http://www.ticahousepublishing.com/amish-miller.html

About the Author

Hannah Miller has been writing Amish Romance for the past seven years. Long intrigued by the Amish way of life, Hannah has traveled the United States, visiting different Amish communities. She treasures her Amish friends and enjoys visiting with them. Hannah makes her home in Indiana, along with her husband, Robert. Together, they have three children and seven grandchildren. Hannah loves to ride bikes in the sunshine. And if it's warm enough for a picnic, you'll find her under the nearest tree!

Made in the USA
Monee, IL
08 May 2020